RENATO
and the
LION

by **Barbara DiLorenzo**

Viking

For my son, Rennie B.,
who showed me that with a little bit of magic, stone lions come alive.

And for Tracy Gates,
who brought the words of this story to life.

Without you both, this story would remain a collection of notes and sketches.

VIKING
An imprint of Penguin Random House LLC
375 Hudson Street
New York, New York 10014

First published in the United States of America by Viking,
an imprint of Penguin Random House LLC, 2017

LIBRARY OF CONGRESS CATALOGING-IN-PUBLICATION DATA IS AVAILABLE
ISBN: 9780451476418

Set in Ambigue Com Regular   Printed in China

10 9 8 7 6 5 4 3 2 1

Acknowledgments

I'd like to thank Enrico Rossi, a bookseller who shared his experience as a young boy in Florence during WWII, and Antonia Lanza
d'Ajeta for translating during our interview. Stefano Veloci at the Pitti Palace kindly gave me books that had photos of art being covered
in Florence during the war. At Princeton University Library, Peter Bae tirelessly helped me search for information on whether or not our
lion was, in fact, covered. Trudy Jacoby, at Princeton's Department of Art and Archaeology, offered photos from the A. Sheldon Pennoyer
Collection which helped me in my visual research. Daniela Turner recalled her experiences as a young girl in WWII Florence which
helped me understand the vague feeling of fear a child might experience during this time. Restaurateur Doris Schechter (shown with curly
hair in the illustration of the ship) offered information on the passage to New York as a young child. Books by art historians Elena Franchi
and Ilaria Dagnini Brey opened my eyes to the protection of art. Dr. Claudio DiBenedetto and the Uffizi Library assisted in the search for
whether the Medici lion was protected. Paolo de Anna sent me lists from the 1940s when Superintendent Poggi cataloged where different
works of art were hidden during the war, so I could rule out that the lion was ever moved.

I'd also like to thank my generous critique group and Italian family members that offered support and assistance whenever I asked.
Thank you especially to Priscilla Mackie for bringing me to Florence for the first time in 1995, and to Renato A. DiLorenzo for bringing me
back over and over again. Thank you to my family, my agent Rachel Orr, and the amazing team at Viking for making this book a reality.

Renato loved his home in Florence, Italy.
He loved the people there. And the food there.
But he especially loved the art there.
It was everywhere.

It was on the walls and ceilings of the churches,
and in the rooms where the friars once slept.

It was around every corner, and in every piazza,
and in the museum where his father worked.

Renato's father cared for artwork called sculptures.
They were made of stone and some had been carved hundreds of years ago.
Sometimes Renato watched his father carefully repair a sculpture when it
had been damaged.

Renato's favorite sculpture wasn't in a museum.
It was in the Piazza della Signoria and it was a stone lion.

He said *buongiorno*—hello—to it every day on his way to school.
After school, Renato and his friends played soccer near the lion.
Later, Renato would walk home with his father.
Buona sera—good evening—they said to the lion.

But one day, Renato's father was late and he looked very tired.
His father took Renato's hand. "I want to show you something, Renato."
And the two of them walked back toward the museum.

In the place where a large sculpture called *David* had been was now
a tall domed wall. "The sculpture is still there," explained his father,
"but if you can't see it, you might not know it was there."
"Who might not know?" asked Renato.
Renato's father pointed out a window.

A group of soldiers was walking down the street.

Renato knew there was a war on in most of Europe.

The fighting was far away, but there were soldiers in Florence,

and military planes often flew across the sky.

"The artwork could be damaged if it's not protected," said his father.

"But we will be here to protect it," said Renato.

His father shook his head. "We are leaving," his father said.

"I need to protect *you*."

Renato swallowed hard. He had friends who had left.

"Where are we going?" he asked.

"Across the ocean," his father answered, "to be with your uncle and his family."

"But what about the lion?" Renato said. "We need to protect him, too."

"We don't have time," said his father. "We must leave tomorrow."

Renato looked around the museum.

He looked at the walled enclosures where the sculptures had been.

Before his father could object, Renato ran toward the piazza.

The lion was standing quietly in the moonlight.

Renato found some bricks like the ones used to protect the sculptures in the museum.
He was putting a few near the lion's paws when he heard the soldiers enter the piazza.
Quickly, Renato pulled himself up on top of the lion's back and made himself small
so he couldn't be seen.

The soldiers stopped nearby and talked in a
language Renato didn't understand.
Renato shut his eyes and breathed quietly.
Before long, he had fallen asleep.

It was the lion's whiskers that woke him,
and the lion's muscles underneath his body
as they padded down the street.
Renato grasped the mane, holding himself on.
The streets of Florence were quiet.

They walked by the fountain of Neptune,

across the Vasari Corridor,

over the Ponte Vecchio,

through the Boboli Gardens,

and then around the corner to his house
where he slid down the lion's back
and into his father's arms.

"We need to protect him,"
Renato said. "He protected me."
But when he turned back to the lion,
he was gone.

"We will protect him," said his father.
He put a hand on Renato's shoulder.
"But first you need to sleep."

In the morning, suitcases were packed into a car
and Renato's family squeezed in beside them.
"Where is Papa?" asked Renato.
"We are picking him up in the piazza," answered his mother.

Papa was waiting for them.
But the lion had disappeared!
Papa held out something in his hands.
It was a brick, like the ones in the walls
at the museum.
And that's when Renato realized—
there was now a wall around his lion.
He took the brick and put it with the others.

"*Grazie,*" Renato said
to the lion,
and to his father,
and to Florence.
Thank you.

A few days later, Renato climbed the gangplank
to the boat that would take them across the ocean.
And many days after that, they landed on a
small island near a big city.

There were so many new things in America that Renato almost forgot his lion. His family moved into a tiny apartment, but Renato loved exploring the big city, and the museums where he could look at paintings and sculptures that reminded him of home.

Years passed. Renato married and had a son,
and that son had a daughter.
One day, Renato walked with his granddaughter
near a large public library.

"Can I pet the lion?" she asked, pointing at one of the
stone lions on the stairs to the library entrance.
Renato nodded and smiled.
"Of course," he said.

"I once knew a lion," he added.
And he told her the story.

His granddaughter's eyes grew wide.
"Is he still there?" she asked.
Renato shrugged. He didn't know.
He had never been back.
"We have to go!" she said.
Renato looked back at the lion, and then nodded—
maybe it was time.

The trip to Florence took less than a day,
many days less than it had coming to
America. So much had changed,
and yet so much hadn't.

The statues in the museum were still there.
And the beautiful frescoes in the friars' rooms.
And the Ponte Vecchio and Boboli Gardens.

Renato took his granddaughter's hand as they walked into the Piazza della Signoria.

Children were playing soccer just as he had as a boy.
He felt a tug on his hand.
His granddaughter was pointing.

She was smiling,
and now so was Renato.
"*Grazie*," he said
to his granddaughter,
to his father,
to Florence.
And to the lion.
Thank you.

Author's Note

My family visited Florence, Italy, when our son was three years old. He was terrified of one of the lions in the Bargello Museum, convinced that it was alive. Despite our reassurances that the lion was made of stone, he wholly believed it was a living, breathing creature. I credit that moment with the birth of this story. Years later, I watched *The Rape of Europa*, a documentary that revealed how the citizens of France and Italy protected their artistic treasures during World War II. I was moved by a photo of Michelangelo's *David*, encased in a brick tomb to protect it from potential bombing. The photo haunted me, and suddenly the connection between a boy, a lion, and Italian history all came together in the form of a story.

I could not know then how many incredible facts and details would reveal themselves to enrich this story. For example, the boat that delivers Renato and his family to America is based on the *Henry Gibbins*, the one and only transport ordered by President Roosevelt to rescue refugees from Europe. It traveled from Naples to New York, and survived bombardment surrounded by a convoy. There were two Renatas and two Renates on the ship's register, so Renato's name made sense. I met one of the young passengers, who grew up to run a restaurant in New York City. I included a portrait on page 31 of Ruth Gruber (holding a camera on the ship's deck), the woman who organized the mission.

I also learned that priceless Italian artwork was moved several times during WWII to keep it as safe as possible. Often statues were covered in different types of materials at different points in time. Although records were kept about what art was placed where, many records were destroyed in the Arno River flood of 1966. There is no record of moving or covering the Medici lion featured in this story, but it survived the war along with its older feline companion, and both still flank the entrance to the Loggia dei Lanzi, next to the Uffizi.

While there are many historical details on which this story is based, I did take liberties with timing and some details for the sake of visual and literary storytelling. For instance, when the passengers of the *Henry Gibbins* disembarked in America, they were transported to a refugee camp in upstate New York. A child like Renato would not have been able to live in New York City until after the war. I also purposely kept the lineage of Renato vague. Europeans fled wartime Europe for various reasons, and Renato is not based on any one personal experience.

Renato and the Lion is a work of fiction first, but after doing all the fascinating research I hope that its many real details will inspire readers to learn more about the world, history, and art.

⚜   ⚜   ⚜